MICE
of the
SEVEN SEAS

TIM DAVIS

Bob Jones University Press, Greenville, South Carolina 29614

Library of Congress Cataloging-in-Publication Data

Davis, Tim, 1957-
    Mice of the Seven Seas / Tim Davis.
       p.   cm.
    Sequel to: Mice of the Nine Lives.
    Summary: When they learn that pirate seadogs have stolen the
Queen's secret orders, two brave mice set out to rescue the Admiral's
expedition to find the legendary Great Continent of the South.
    ISBN 0-89084-845-9
    [1. Pirates—Fiction. 2. Mice—Fiction. 3. Cats—Fiction.
4. Dogs—Fiction.]   I. Title.
PZ7.D3179Mip   1995
[E]—dc20   95–36840
                                          CIP
                                          AC

Mice of the Seven Seas

Edited by Debbie L. Parker

Cover and illustrations by Tim Davis

© 1995 Bob Jones University Press
Greenville, South Carolina 29614

ISBN 0-89084-845-9

15 14 13 12 11 10 9 8 7 6 5 4 3 2

To my very own crew—

Katie, Stephen, and Christiana—

helping me sail the seas of imagination

every day

Books illustrated by Tim Davis
Pocket Change
Grandpa's Gizmos
The Cranky Blue Crab

Books written and illustrated by Tim Davis
Mice of the Herring Bone
Mice of the Nine Lives
Mice of the Seven Seas

Contents

Chapter One
Her Majesty's Mission

Oliver nudged his friend. "Pssst, Charles. How do I look? Are my whiskers straight?"

"Believe me, Oliver, you've never looked better," said Charles. He smoothed his own whiskers and adjusted his collar.

The two mice stood in front of a giant wooden door. On it were carved dozens of figures that told of royal battles. There were lions with crowns upon their heads, knights fighting dragons, and beautiful princesses. In the middle was carved a large seal—the seal of the Queen. Oliver stepped forward to look at it more closely.

"This is marvelous," he said.

"Be careful, mate," said a voice behind him. It was Mr. Calico, the first mate of the *Nine Lives*. "Those dragons are nearly as big as you are."

Next to Mr. Calico stood Admiral Winchester, his head held high. He was already one of the top-ranking cats in the Royal Navy. But this was a special honor indeed—to appear before the Queen herself!

"Pssst, Admiral," whispered Oliver. "How will we know when it's time to go in?"

The Admiral smiled. "You need not worry, Oliver. They will open the doors and announce us."

"Don't forget to bow," Charles reminded his friend.

Suddenly the giant doors whooshed open in front of them. The force of the air nearly pulled Charles and Oliver down on their faces. Before they had regained their footing, the sound of a trumpet blast filled their ears. *Ta-ra-ta-ra!*

The herald announced them. "Your Majesty, I present unto you the honorable Admiral Winchester of the *Nine Lives*. With him, I present his brave first mate, Mr. Calico. And finally, Charles and Oliver, the heroic mice of the *Herring Bone*."

Another trumpet blast rang through the hall. The four friends walked forward, down a long red carpet toward the throne. Oliver couldn't help looking around. The ceiling above was so high and so beautiful! It was decorated with flowing designs that swirled across long arches.

Golden statues of creatures and kings peered down from the walls. And banners of blue, purple, and scarlet hung between the statues, filling the great room with color.

"Wow!" whispered Oliver.

Charles poked him in the ribs. "Bow!" he whispered.

Oliver looked ahead. The Queen! He bowed as gracefully as his round stomach would allow.

"My dear heroic friends," the Queen began. "Let me offer you my sincere thanks. First, we commend you for your courageous work in recovering lost treasures from under the sea. Second, we thank you for recapturing the *Seven Seas* from those scourges of the Cattibean, the sea dogs of Captain Crag."

The Queen paused, and the Commander of the Royal Navy pulled four golden medals out of a small treasure chest. The medals sparkled brightly on their scarlet ribbons.

The Queen continued. "In honor of your great bravery and your loyalty to the throne, I hereby present each of you with the Queen's Medal of Courage. May you wear it ever as a token of my gratitude."

The Commander placed a medal around the neck of each mouse and each cat. The four friends bowed before the Queen. The trumpets gave a loud blast: *Ta-ra, Ta-ra!* Then all the attendants in the throne room clapped loudly. The Queen smiled down at Oliver and Charles.

Though the gold medal nearly covered his chest, Oliver had never felt so big. He imagined he could almost touch the ceiling.

The Queen spoke again. "Admiral Winchester, I have a special request of you."

"Only name it," replied the Admiral.

"In recognition of your accomplished service," said the Queen, "I hereby request that you command the *Nine Lives* and her crew on a most important mission. I wish you to search for the legendary Great Continent of the South. Should you find this mysterious land, you may claim it on behalf of my royal person and our great Empire."

The Admiral bowed gracefully. "Your Majesty," he said, "I consider your offer of this mission my highest honor, and I humbly accept your most gracious request."

Several hushed "Ooohs" and "Aaahhs" sounded through the hall.

The Queen smiled. "Then you shall leave on the morrow, Admiral. May your mission be a success. Let the Great Southern Continent, if it truly exists, become a part of the greatest Empire under the sun."

She picked up a folder of papers and slid it into a red silk packet. Both sides of the packet were stamped with the Queen's own gold seal.

She handed the red packet to Admiral Winchester.

"These are my orders," said the Queen. "They contain all the details of your mission. In them you will find the fastest route to your destination. This information is known only to the Royal Commander and to myself. Take care that it does not fall into the wrong hands."

"Thank you, your Majesty," said Admiral Winchester.

The Queen smiled warmly. "Go with my blessing!"

The four heroes were dismissed with a great fanfare of trumpets. They walked back down the red carpet. As they stepped out of the throne room, the tall wooden doors closed behind them.

"Wow!" was all Oliver could say.

Admiral Winchester looked down at the two mice. "My friends, I hope you will come with us to search for the Great Southern Continent."

"Hmm." Oliver scratched his head. "Maybe a trip south would be nice. The nights are getting cold around here."

Charles laughed. "Oliver, you must not know how far south they're going."

"It's nearly to the South Pole, mate!" Mr. Calico added.

Oliver shivered. "No thank you, then."

"I think I'm ready to retire from life at sea, Captain," said Charles. "But we wish you the best of success. What an honor to be selected!"

The Admiral frowned a little. "Surely you will at least see us off at the docks?"

"Most certainly," replied the two mice.

"Come then, Mr. Calico, for we have much to do before tomorrow." The Admiral and his first mate went their way with the Queen's sealed orders in hand.

The next morning, Charles and Oliver rose early to go down to the docks and say good-bye. Sea gulls squawked everywhere. Sailors hurried all about, loading barrels, boxes, and other supplies. Dozens of ships seemed to be getting ready to go to sea.

The two mice scurried around, trying to stay out from underfoot. They scrambled up onto a barrel near the *Nine Lives*. "We've got a good view from here," said Charles.

"Let's just stay out of this barrel,"said Oliver, "or we might be taking an unplanned sea voyage." The two mice chuckled and smiled at each other.

Admiral Winchester and Mr. Calico hurried over to say good-bye. "It's going to be an exciting adventure," said the Admiral. "Are you sure you won't reconsider my invitation?"

"Thank you, but no, my dear friend," said Charles.

"I'd rather not become an icicle," said Oliver.

"Good-bye, then," said both cats.

"Farewell," said the mice, and the cats returned to the ship for their final preparations.

Before long, the *Nine Lives* pushed off from the dock and unfurled its large white sails.

Wind filled the sails of the great ship, and it swept out to sea.

From their perch atop the barrel, Charles and Oliver watched their friends sail away.

"It's a beautiful morning for sailing," Charles said with a sigh.

"It sure is," replied Oliver. He gazed up into the sky at the sea gulls swooping up and down behind the *Nine Lives*. From among the graceful white birds, another, more clumsy bird came flapping back toward the docks.

"Look," said Oliver, "a parrot."

"Caw, caw."

"Looks like it's carrying something in its claws," said Charles.

"That bird . . . it looks familiar."

"Barnacle!" cried Charles. "The sea dogs' parrot!"

"And he's got the Admiral's plans in his claws!" cried Oliver. "Look—the Queen's gold seal!"

Chapter Two
The Chase

Charles and Oliver stared up at the squawking parrot. "We've got to do something!" cried Charles. "That bird will take those secret plans back to Captain Crag and his gang of sea dogs!"

"Maybe we can warn Admiral Winchester," said Oliver.

"It's too late for that," said Charles. "The *Nine Lives* is under full sail and headed out to sea. We could never catch it. But maybe, just maybe, we can catch that bird! Come on!"

He grabbed Oliver by the paw and scurried down the barrel. They hustled along the busy docks, dodging the feet of sailors and fishermen.

"I'll keep an eye on that bird," said Charles, looking up at the sky. "You keep us from running into anything."

Oliver tightened his grip on his friend's paw. "I'll do my best."

The two mice ran full speed along the dock. Charles yelled out directions to Oliver. Oliver yelled out directions to Charles. They dashed through a maze of legs, ropes, and barrels.

"Faster!" yelled Charles. "We're losing ground!"

"It's no wonder," said Oliver. "That bird's got nothing to dodge up there!"

"At least he doesn't seem to notice we're following him," said Charles. "I'm sure he'd be flying faster if he did."

"Phew!" Oliver panted.

"That way!" shouted Charles. And they turned a corner away from the docks and into town.

The street was full of traffic—horse-drawn carriages, merchants' wagons, even sheep being herded to market. Charles kept watching the bird ahead, and they charged down the middle of the noisy street.

Oliver shouted out directions as fast as he could. "Right! . . . Left!" *Clippety-clop, clippety-clop.* "Look out!" *Baaaaah, baaaaah!* It took all his strength to pull Charles away from the sheep's hooves and rolling cart wheels.

Far ahead of them, the parrot disappeared into a cloud of black smoke. "We're losing him!" Charles gasped.

They heard a clanging behind them. Voices shouted, "Firewagon's coming! Clear a way!" *Clang, clang!* Oliver looked back. A wagon pulled by galloping horses was speeding down the middle of the street—right toward them.

"Charles!" he yelled.

"It's no use," sighed Charles, still staring at the smoke down the street. "We've lost him."

Clang! claNG! cLANG!! CLANG!!! The galloping horses charged closer and closer.

"Look what's coming!" squeaked Oliver. He jerked his friend away from the pounding hooves.

"Hey! We'll grab a ride!" shouted Charles.

"You're crazy!" yelled Oliver.

But Charles clutched at Oliver's tail and leaped toward the passing wagon. He landed on the spoke of one wheel.

"Ooof!" Somehow he held on. Charles wrapped all four legs around the wooden spoke. He was spinning around in circles, still tightly gripping Oliver's tail. Oliver was flying round and round in circles, too.

"HELP!" yelled Oliver. "Charles, help!"

"I've got you! We're catching up!" But Charles couldn't hold on any longer. Both mice flew off the wheel, high into the air.

"YEEEEEOOOOOOOOWEEEEE!" cried Oliver.

20

They passed through the black cloud of smoke and arched back down toward the city below. Charles still held onto Oliver's tail as they tumbled through the air. Oliver didn't dare open his eyes.

THWAP! They slapped into a wet cloth. It was a sheet hanging out to dry on a rooftop clothesline. They rolled down it and—*thwap!* onto another clothesline below.

"Ouch! My tail!" cried Oliver. "It's caught!" He kicked against the sheet and stared up at his tail, which seemed to be hooked over the clothesline. Where was Charles?

"Are you all right?" His friend's voice came from the other side of the sheet.

"Oh, you must be the one who's squeezing my tail," said Oliver.

"Sorry," said Charles. "But your tail is the only thing keeping us up here. Shouldn't you grab hold of something first?"

Oliver looked down into the narrow alley, three stories beneath them. "Good idea," he said.

Just then they heard a commotion in the alley below.

"What's that?" asked Oliver, still dangling upside down.

"Somebody's coming," said Charles.

"Maybe they can help us get down so I don't land on my head," said Oliver.

"Let me try." As Charles struggled to pull them both up onto the clothesline, they heard voices.

Two sailors were shouting at each other, down in the alley. "I'll wager yer bird flied the coop," a big sailor sneered.

" 'E's around someplace," said the other. "I tell ya, my bird's as loyal as they come."

Oliver took a firm grip on the clothesline. "Thank you," he whispered to Charles. "My tail feels much better already."

The big sailor shook his head and growled loudly. "What der you know 'bout birds, O'Grady, except maybe how their brains werk—like yers." He laughed, a great big barking laugh.

Oliver looked over at Charles. Charles looked back at him.

"Crag's pirates!" they whispered together.

Meanwhile, the sea dogs below looked as if they were about to start a fight. Suddenly another sea dog ran up the alley toward them.

"No time fer fightin', mates," he called. "Cap'n Crag warnts ye back inside."

"Fer what?" growled the big sea dog.

"Yer bird's come back from the docks with a prize, O'Grady. The Cap'n warnts ye in on it."

O'Grady started bragging about his pet parrot, and the three sea dogs shuffled down the alley.

Charles sprang into action. He grabbed a handkerchief that was hanging on the line. "This will make us a nice parachute," he said.

Then, with each of them holding onto two corners, they parachuted into the alley below.

"Whooaa!" cried Oliver.

They floated clumsily through the air and landed in a heap on the ground.

"Are you all right, Oliver?" asked Charles.

"I think so." Oliver dusted himself off.

"Then come on," said Charles. "Let's follow those sea dogs!"

They scampered over the cobblestones and back into another narrow, dark alley. The pirates were just closing a rickety door behind them. "Up here!" whispered Charles.

He hurried up the bricks to the sooty edge of a window, and Oliver followed. From there they could hear a rough, tough voice they knew. It was the mean old bulldog himself, Captain Crag.

"See 'ere mates, whart Barnacle 'as brought us is orders from the Queenie 'erself." Crag chuckled with glee. "She's sent ar dear Admiral Winchester an' the crew of the *Nine Lives* ta explore the Great Continent of the South. An' we got the secret route an' all, right 'ere!"

Sea dogs all around growled their approval, and Barnacle the parrot puffed out his chest. He cawed proudly.

"So, Cap'n," said the sea dog named Big Tom, "does we get another chance at them cats?"

"Aye, mates," Crag said. "An' that's not all. Thar's talk of treasures buried in the ice on that thar continent. If they finds treasure, then we'll makes sure we takes it off thar hands, see? Har, har, har."

O'Grady's wooden leg started tapping the floor with excitement.

Big Tom growled at him. "Quit yer tappin' O'Grady." He turned to Crag. "When we leavin', Cap'n?"

"We sets sail on the *Red Herring* at midnight, mates," said Crag. "Now I know it'll warm yer hearts ta drown those cats in the icy water, but till then, be sure yer ready fer some mighty cold weather, see?"

"An' whart about those mice?" snarled O'Grady. "Will we get ar chance at them, Cap'n?"

Through the dingy glass, Oliver could see Captain Crag smile and stroke his stubbly chin. "I hope so, mates. I do hope so."

Chapter Three
Back to Sea

"We've got to warn the *Nine Lives!*" squeaked Charles.

"But how can we?" asked Oliver. "They're long gone by now."

"Maybe we could stow away on board the *Red Herring.*"

"Oh no!" said Oliver. "I'm not about to travel on any pirate ship again. I've had enough of that for one lifetime!"

"Maybe there's another ship going that way," said Charles. He grabbed his friend's paw. "Come on. Let's head back to the docks."

"Really now, Charles, how many ships are going to be sailing for an undiscovered continent near the South Pole?"

"Oh, Oliver, I don't know, but there's got to be some way. Let's just go look!"

They hurried back through the busy streets and down to the docks. There they scampered from ship to ship. Charles questioned everyone who looked ready to sail, but nobody was going south. The two mice were about to give up when they recognized a familiar ship—the *Seven Seas*! And there on deck was none other than their old friend, Captain Tabby.

"Charles! Oliver! How good to see you again!" shouted the tall striped cat. "I heard about the Queen's ceremony honoring your bravery. Congratulations!"

Oliver looked down shyly. "Thank you."

Charles smiled. "Thank you," he said.

Captain Tabby invited his two small friends on board and they shook paws with him. The tall cat smiled. "My good mice, I can never thank you enough for your help in getting my ship back from Crag and his scoundrels. If there's ever anything I can do for you, don't hesitate to ask."

"Hmmm," Charles said thoughtfully. "Actually, there is one favor we'd like to ask."

"Only name it," said Captain Tabby.

Oliver took a deep breath. "It's just that we need a ship to take us to the Great Continent of the South—so we can warn the Admiral and the *Nine Lives* about Crag and his sea dogs—

they're going to follow them and attack their ship and steal any treasure they might find and drown them in the icy water near the South Pole."

Captain Tabby stared down at the two mice. Finally he said, "Is that all?"

The mice nodded.

"Let's go then!" he said.

"Admiral Winchester told us his route before he left," said Charles, "so we can be your navigators!"

"Wonderful!" exclaimed Captain Tabby.

Before the afternoon was half over, the *Seven Seas*, complete with a crew that included two mice as guides, set sail for the Great Continent of the South.

The winds were favorable, and the *Seven Seas* had smooth sailing for several days. Every morning Charles and Oliver climbed up to the crow's-nest of the ship. They took turns peering through the small spyglass Captain Tabby had given them. First, they looked north, then south, east, west, and everywhere in between, but they saw no sign of the *Nine Lives* or of the *Red Herring*.

The ship passed through the warm currents near the equator and continued southward. Still they saw no other ships. They stopped near the southern tip of Africa for fresh supplies and asked about other ships. A ship called the *Nine Lives* had left port just the day before.

"At least we're on the right track," said Captain Tabby. "With some more fair weather

and favorable winds we may catch them yet!"
The *Seven Seas* left port as soon as it was
loaded.

Three days later, Charles and Oliver started
up to the crow's-nest right after breakfast, as
usual. The sky was filled with dark gray clouds.
Halfway up the rigging, Oliver stopped to turn
up his collar.

"Hold on tight, mate," called Charles, just
above him on the ropes. "There's a mighty stiff
breeze this morning!"

"And it's cold, too!" said Oliver.

"Better get used to that," said Charles. "It
will only be getting colder from here on."

"Brrrr. That thought doesn't make me feel
any better."

"At least we're making good time in this wind," said Charles. "Maybe we're catching up to the *Nine Lives*. Let's take a look."

Oliver held the spyglass, while Charles peered through. Then they switched off, and Oliver took his turn. He squeaked with glee.

"A ship! A ship, Charles! I see a ship!"

"Where?" asked Charles, squinting out at the ocean.

"There!" squeaked Oliver. "Here, you look!"

"I see it!" shouted Charles. "Let's go! We've got to tell Captain Tabby the good news!"

Oliver had turned in another direction. He took another look through the spyglass. "Wait a minute," he said slowly. "If that's the *Nine Lives*—then what's that ship back there?"

"Huh?" Charles grabbed for the spyglass, nearly knocking Oliver off his feet.

"What can you see?" asked Oliver.

Charles groaned. "A black flag, with red fish bones."

"Oh, no!" cried Oliver. "The *Red Herring*!"

"I'm afraid they've caught up to us." Charles said. "Let's find the Captain."

The two mice crawled cautiously down the rigging toward the deck below. The ropes twisted in the strong wind. Oliver looked back up at the sky. The clouds were growing lower and darker. By the time they reached the deck, sailors were scurrying around, trimming sails, and tying down anything that was loose. They found Captain Tabby in the middle of everyone, shouting out orders to the crew.

"Captain! Captain!" Charles shouted over the wind and commotion. "We've spotted the *Nine Lives!*"

"And the *Red Herring!*" added Oliver.

"At such a time!" Captain Tabby looked worried. "Well, there's nothing we can do about it now, mates. We've got to ride out this storm. Better head back to my cabin. I'll join you when I can."

A few hours later, the soaking wet captain joined his mice friends in the Captain's quarters. "Tea is ready," said Charles. He had used some hot coals from the captain's footwarmer to heat it.

Oliver was lying on a pillow. He held his stomach and groaned as the ship pitched back and forth in the waves.

"Looks like we'll be holed up for a while," said the dripping cat. "We've got high seas. And those are gale-force winds out there. No sign of letting up."

Oliver groaned again.

"Think we'll lose track of the *Nine Lives*?" asked Charles.

"Quite possible, mate," said Captain Tabby. "A storm like this can set ships at sea in a scramble." He stirred his tea and watched it swirl. "There's no telling where we'll all come out."

Chapter Four
Feathered
Friends

After several dark, stormy days, the sun broke through the clouds. The sea calmed. Captain Tabby and his crew unfurled the sails of the *Seven Seas* to catch the cold morning breeze.

"Brrrrrrrr." Oliver shivered. "How much colder is it going to get?"

"I don't know," said Charles. "But my tea from yesterday was frozen in the pot this morning. How are you feeling, Oliver?"

"A lot better, now that the waves aren't so big."

"Are you feeling up to a trip into the crow's-nest?" asked Charles.

"Certainly!" said Oliver. "I want to know where those ships are—as much as you do."

The two mice carried their little spyglass high up into the crow's-nest. Oliver took his turn first, peering ahead to the south.

"See anything?" asked Charles.

"Yes!" said Oliver. "Something white."

"A sail?" asked Charles.

"I don't think so," said Oliver. "It looks more like a mountain . . . a floating white mountain."

Charles took a look. "An iceberg! Captain Tabby said we'd be seeing some soon."

"An ice what?"

"Iceberg. A great big chunk of ice floating in the sea," said Charles. "We should be coming into a whole bunch of them quite soon."

Oliver sighed. "I thought it was cold enough already. Now we've got ice to keep the water really cold!"

"Oliver, it means we're getting closer. If the Great Southern Continent really exists, it's somewhere beyond that field of ice."

For days, the *Seven Seas* worked its way through a maze of icebergs. Every day the mountains of ice seemed to grow bigger. Many of them were taller than the ship itself. The air grew frostier. Some mornings they sailed through an icy mist.

"How are we ever going to find the *Nine Lives* now?" asked Oliver. "We're practically surrounded by towering iceburbs, not to mention the fog!"

"*Bergs*, Oliver. Icebergs," said Charles.

"Whatever you want to call them, we can hardly see any distance at all," said Oliver.

Captain Tabby's voice called from behind them. "You've got a point, my good mouse. That's precisely why we're going to anchor over there—between those two icebergs."

The two mice looked at each other, puzzled.

Captain Tabby pointed ahead to a passageway between two gigantic icy islands. "After we anchor," he said, "I'll row the skiff over to the biggest iceberg and climb up to the top."

"We should get a good view, once the mist clears. Would you like to join me?"

"Why not?" they said together.

Before long the three friends were huffing and puffing up the snow-covered slopes of the giant iceberg. They had just about reached the uppermost ridge when they heard footsteps on the other side—hundreds of footsteps! And not only that—there were squeals and screams.

"What's that?" asked Oliver, with wide eyes.

"The crew of the *Nine Lives*?" asked Charles. "Or the sea dogs?"

"Only one way to find out," said Captain Tabby. "Come on."

Cautiously, they peered over the top of the ridge. Penguins! Hundreds of penguins!

The black and white birds waddled back and forth, slipping and sliding on the ice. A line of them came trudging up the hill. Each one in turn plopped himself down at the top of an icy track, and *whoosh*—he slid down the slippery slope at full speed. The other penguins cheered and chirped as they watched.

"They look rather harmless," said the Captain. "Maybe they can be of help to us."

He stepped over the ridge. "Hello," he called.

Soon the three friends were surrounded by curious penguins. The birds clucked with excitement and asked them all kinds of questions.

"Who are you?"

"What are you?"

"Where did you come from?"

"Do you want to go sliding?"

"What are you looking for?"

"There's the question," said Captain Tabby. "We're looking for a ship."

"A ship?"

"What's a ship?"

"How do you spell that?"

Oliver began, "S-H—um—let's see—"

Charles sighed. "Never mind, it doesn't matter. Come over here, and I'll show you one."

He led the excited birds back up to the top of the icy ridge. Anchored far below them was the *Seven Seas*. "That," said Charles, "is a ship."

The penguins cheered with glee.

"The ship! He found the ship!"

"Good show! He found the ship!"

"So that is a ship. What a marvelous ship!"

"No, no," said Captain Tabby. "That is not the ship we are looking for. We are looking for another ship."

"Is that one broken?"

"Can we help you fix it?"

"Another ship, yes, I have seen another ship," said one plump penguin.

"You have?" Oliver asked.

"Where did you see it?" asked the Captain.

"At the other end of the iceberg," replied the penguin.

"Did you see its flag?" asked the Captain.

"Flag?"

"What is a flag?"

"How do you spell that?"

Oliver scratched his head. "Let's see, F-L . . . uh—"

"Never mind," said the Captain. "Could you take my two friends over to see that other ship?"

"Certainly!" replied the helpful penguin.

"Good!" said Captain Tabby. "I'll head back to the *Seven Seas* and get her ready to take up anchor." He looked at the mice. "Return to the ship with your report."

"Aye, aye, Captain!" they said together.

The friends went their separate ways. Oliver and Charles introduced themselves to the penguin who had seen the other ship.

"Nice to meet you," he replied. "My name is Perry. If you'd like, we can slide over to the other end of the iceberg. You can ride with me."

"Uh, sure, I guess," said Oliver.

"Why not?" said Charles.

So the plump bird waddled over to the icy track, and the two mice hopped onto his back.

"Hold on tight," said Perry. He plopped down onto the ice. "Here we go."

Whoooosh! The slippery bird slid down the track like a well-greased toboggan. *Swish, swoosh.* They sped down —down—down and around the icy curves.

"Can't you slow down?" yelled Oliver.

"Maybe I could," called Perry, "but it might not be a good idea."

"Why not?" Oliver hung on for dear life.

"Look behind us."

Over his shoulder, Oliver saw a long line of penguins speeding right behind them.

"Things can really get complicated if the leader slows down," said Perry.

They swished and swooshed their way around big banked turns, ducked under snowy tunnels, and curved through Y-turns and exit ramps. Finally they slowed on the other side of the iceberg. Behind them, at least three dozen penguins gently bumped and slid their way to a stop. Then the troop waddled to a high bank overlooking the water.

"There it is," whispered Perry. "Below us."

Charles and Oliver eagerly peered over the edge of the snowbank. To Oliver's dismay, the ship flew the black and red flag of Crag and his flea-bitten crew. The ship was sailing slowly alongside the icy bank.

"Oh, no," sighed Oliver. "Wrong ship!"

The penguins looked puzzled.

"How many of these ships are there?"

"What's wrong with that ship?"

"Can't you use your own ship?"

"I don't think you understand," said Charles. "That ship is filled with sea dogs!"

"Sea dogs?"

"Oh dear! Sea dogs?"

"What are sea dogs?"

"How do you spell that?"

"All you need to know about sea dogs is that they destroy just about everything they can get their hands on," said Charles.

"Do you think they would hurt your ship?" asked Perry.

"I'm sure they would if they could find it," said Oliver.

"Well, they will before long," said Perry. "As soon as they get to the end of the iceberg, they'll see it on the other side."

"Oh no!" said Charles. "The *Seven Seas* is in big trouble! Its cannons are on the sides of the ship, and there's no room for the ship to turn sideways. So it won't be able to shoot at them!"

The penguins looked even more puzzled. Not one of them asked a question.

"What we need to do first," said Oliver, "is stop the sea dogs' ship."

"Oh, stop the ship?"

"Yes, we'll stop the ship!"

"Come on, let's go stop the ship!"

The penguins waddled into action immediately. They made snowballs. Quickly they rolled them over the edge of the bank. As the snowballs rolled down the snow-covered slope, they grew bigger and bigger and bigger—then they smashed into the ship.

"Shiver me timbers!" yelled a voice from below. "It's an avalanche!"

"Whart's goin'—*oooff!*"

"Caw! Caw!"

Thud! Smoosh! Splat! One after another, the giant snowballs crashed onto the deck of the *Red Herring*. They crashed into barrels and cannons and sea dogs. They knocked down sails and covered the deck with snow. The ship slowed down, but it didn't stop.

"Keep up the good work, mates!" Charles called. "Oliver and I must go back to warn the Captain!" And the two mice left the penguins to their snowballing as they hurried back to the *Seven Seas*.

Chapter Five
From Danger to Danger

Oliver and Charles scrambled, slipped, and slid down the other side of the iceberg. By the time they climbed aboard the *Seven Seas*, both of them were out of breath.

"Captain! Captain!" called Oliver. "It's the *Red Herring*! And it's heading this way! Just a couple of minutes—and it'll be up in front. Ready to blast us! We've got to get out of here!"

Captain Tabby pulled at his whiskers. "The wind is behind us," he said. "We can't back up in this narrow passage. And there's not enough room to turn the ship broadside and return fire!"

"Do you mean to say that we're sitting ducks?" Oliver gasped.

"Unless we can back our way out of this, I'm afraid you're right," said the Captain, scratching his head.

"There's got to be some way," said Charles.

"Shall we pull up anchor, Captain?" asked a sailor at the bow.

Captain Tabby was about to answer when suddenly Charles cried out, "That's it!"

"What's it?" asked Oliver.

"We've got two anchors, right, Captain?"

"Right."

"One on each side, right?"

"Right."

"If we were to put them in the skiff, row back behind the ship, and hook one anchor onto each of those big icebergs—"

"And crank them in—to pull the ship back!" finished Captain Tabby. "You know, it just might work!"

Oliver gave Charles an anxious glance. It sounded pretty complicated to him.

"Sailor!" shouted the Captain.

"Aye, Cap'n."

"Bring up that anchor on the double!"

"Aye, aye, sir."

Everyone hurried to follow Captain Tabby's orders. Both anchors were carefully lowered into the skiff, then two burly sailors rowed back behind the *Seven Seas.*

Another sailor let out the rope and made sure it didn't tangle. The skiff had rowed far behind the ship when Oliver saw the *Red Herring* appear in front of them.

A gruff voice bellowed across the water, "Fire the cannons!"

Splat! Splosh! Splish! Snow splattered down onto the deck of the *Seven Seas*.

"What's this?" shouted Captain Tabby.

"Snow, sir," replied the mice.

Splatter! Splish! Splat! Another round of snow-clumps hit the deck.

"Just thank the penguins, Captain!" said Charles with a smile. "All those snowballs must have clogged up the sea dogs' cannons!"

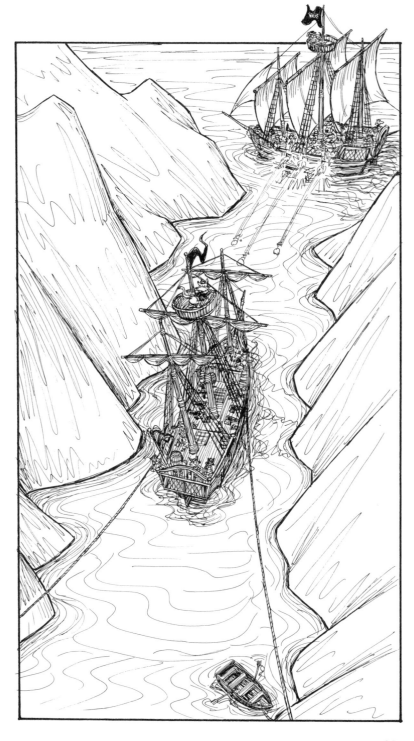

Across the water they heard a grumbling bulldog yell at his crew. "Clean out yer cannons, ya mangy excuses fer sea dogs! This ain't a snowball fight!"

Suddenly the *Seven Seas* lurched backwards as the crew cranked in the anchors.

"It's working!" shouted Oliver. He gave his friend a hug. "Charles, I don't know what we'd do without you!"

"Keep her straight, now, mates," shouted Captain Tabby.

The sailors cranked the ship back through the narrow passageway.

But before they could get away, the cannons of the *Red Herring* boomed again. *Splash! Splash! Splash!* Every cannonball fell into the water in front of the *Seven Seas*.

They were out of range! The whole crew of cats cheered.

"Hurray!"

"Good show!"

Captain Tabby looked over at Charles and winked. "Good job, mate! Looks like you've rescued the *Seven Seas* again!"

Oliver felt very proud to be Charles's friend.

After the crew had cranked the ship all the way out of the passageway between the icebergs, the two sailors loosened the anchors in each iceberg and the crew pulled the anchors in. The Captain let the big ship drift backwards for a while longer. Then the two sailors rowed back to the ship and joined in the celebration.

Once the ship had cleared the icebergs, Captain Tabby gave the command, and the sails were unfurled. But this time they steered a course around the other side of the field of big icebergs.

"Better keep on your guard," warned the Captain. "We could cross paths with the *Red Herring* again. They might appear around an iceberg at any minute."

The crew kept watch for any sign of the sea dogs, and they kept the cannons at the ready. But the mist was settling in again, and they could see no sign of the pirate ship as they crept past the floating mountains of ice.

After a while most of the crew settled down for the night. Sleep came easily to the tired mice, and they huddled under a blanket in Captain Tabby's quarters.

Near morning, Oliver was half-awakened by the sound of groans and whistles. He poked his friend and muttered, "Charles, you're snoring."

"Huh?" Charles rolled over in bed.

Oliver heard more groans and whistles. He poked his friend again. "Charles!"

"It's not me," said Charles. He sat up. "Listen."

Oliver sat up too and listened. "It's getting louder."

"It sounds like it's coming from below," Charles said.

"You think the whole crew is snoring together?" asked Oliver.

"No," answered Charles, "I think it's coming from under the ship!"

The two mice put on their coats and went out on deck to look over the ship's rail.

"I don't see anything," said Oliver. He peered into the dim light of dawn.

Then off in the distance came a loud splash. "What was that?" asked Oliver.

They heard more splashes, each one closer. Waves slapped against the side of the ship.

"Whales!" came a cry from the sailor on guard. "Headed this way!"

Suddenly, something leaped out of the water, right next to the ship. It looked like nothing Oliver had ever seen. Its head was enormous, all black and white. The whale sank back into the water. *KER-SPLASH!* The ship rocked in a gigantic wave.

Both mice lost their balance and teetered on the rail. Oliver grabbed the rigging, but Charles tumbled into the dark sea.

"Charles!" cried Oliver.

Just then the ship shook from a mighty thud. It had been hit! A whole school of whales was passing under and around the ship. One of them must have rammed into the hull.

"Man the pumps!" shouted Captain Tabby. "We're taking in water fast!"

The ship's crew sprang into action. Some worked at the pumps while others lightened the ship to keep it from sinking so fast. It was a bad leak. If the *Seven Seas* was to stay afloat, it would only be through the heroic efforts of every hand on board.

Oliver hung onto the rail, searching the
churning waters below. Finally the whales
passed and the waves died down.

Oliver scurried along the railing, all the way
around the ship. He stared down into the water
as he ran. Where was Charles? "Help! Help!"
he cried. "Someone help Charles!"

But everyone was busy, and his voice was lost in the commotion. Once again he searched the dark sea below. There was no sign of Charles.

Chapter Six
Barely Afloat

Oliver crept behind a barrel and curled up with his paws over his eyes. The *Seven Seas* was sinking. Charles was lost somewhere in the sea.

"Why did we ever come on this voyage?" he said to himself. "We haven't found the Great Southern Continent. We haven't even found the *Nine Lives*. Charles is sunk, and the rest of us are sinking!"

He felt like crying. But then he had a thought. What if *he'd* been washed overboard, not Charles? Would Charles just give up?

Would Charles sit down and cry at a time like this? *No!* Charles wouldn't give up. And neither would he!

Oliver smoothed his fur and stepped back out onto the noisy deck. He'd find out what he could do to help save the ship.

The Captain was directing sailors to roll the cannons and heavier items overboard. "We'll save her yet," he cried. "Stay at the pumps!"

Oliver had to stand on tiptoe and shout so the Captain would hear him. "Reporting for duty, Sir. What can I do?"

"Can you swim?" asked the Captain.

"A little."

"We need to stop up that hole in the hull, but I can't spare anyone to dive under the ship.

It may be dangerous. Are you willing to try?"

Oliver gulped. "Aye, Captain."

Captain Tabby pulled out his knife and rushed up the rigging. He cut down a large sail. *Fwop!* It fell to the deck. Quickly he tied a rope onto one corner of the sail and a second rope to another corner of the sail. Then he tied the other end of the rope to a burlap sack. He put a big cannonball in the sack.

Chills ran down Oliver's spine. He opened his mouth to ask about the sack. But he closed it hurriedly as the ship began to creak. It tilted slowly to one side.

"She's fillin' up, Cap'n," shouted a sailor. "We don't have much longer!"

Captain Tabby dashed over to Oliver.

"Here—hold onto this sack. I'm going to toss it overboard. The cannonball will take you and the rope straight down." He pulled out a pocket knife that was nearly as long as Oliver and tucked it through his belt.

"When you're all the way down, cut away the cannonball sack. Then take the rope, swim under the ship, and come up on the other side. When you get to the surface, I'll be there to help you. But remember, once you cut the rope free from the sack, swim as fast as you can. Otherwise you might get sucked into the hole yourself!"

The deck tilted under their feet. "Ready?"

Oliver nodded. He clung to the sack with all four paws, shut his eyes, and took a deep breath. *Whoosh!* Captain Tabby threw the heavy sack over the rail.

Oliver sped down through the icy cold water like a stone. *Yank!* Must be the end of the rope. He opened his eyes and looked up. There was the bottom of the ship. A point of light shone through the hull. What a hole! He sure didn't want to get sucked in through that.

He pulled out the Captain's knife and sawed at the rope. It was tough. He slashed at it again. Almost! The knife slipped out of his paw and disappeared. But the rope still held by a thread. He twisted himself around. He gnawed at the rope. Bubbles streamed up from his mouth. *Snap!* The sack fell into the darkness beneath.

But now he was desperate for air. He swam under the ship, pulling the rope with him and using his last ounce of strength. His lungs ached. At last he shot up to the surface.

He felt himself being snatched out of the water, and he went limp.

Captain Tabby tied Oliver's rope to the mast. "Wrap a blanket around that mouse," he yelled to a sailor. "Good job, mate," he called to Oliver. "Now the crew and I can pull that sail down under the ship and over the hole. It should slow the leak so we can work on the hull from the inside."

Oliver's teeth chattered with cold. "Ch-Ch-Char-Charles . . ." But before he could finish, Captain Tabby rushed off.

Oliver huddled under the blanket, trying to warm up from his icy dive. His body ached with cold. He could hear the crew pumping, repairing, and lightening the ship. It all seemed like a bad dream, as if he weren't really there.

When he woke up, it was morning. He found himself in the Captain's cabin.

"Are you all right?" asked the Captain.

"Er—yes, I think so." said Oliver.

"Much thanks to you, we're still afloat," said Captain Tabby. "We're taking turns at the pumps."

Oliver bit his lip. "Charles went overboard last night," he said.

"Oh no!" said the Captain. "How did you get him out?"

"I never found him."

Captain Tabby put his head in his paws. "Why didn't you tell me sooner?"

"There wasn't time," sniffed Oliver. "Besides, I think the whales got him."

"I'm so sorry, Oliver," said the Captain. He put a gentle paw around Oliver.

After a moment, Oliver asked, "How's the ship, Captain?"

He shook his head. "We've got to find the *Nine Lives*. We'll never be able to get back to England in our condition."

"And what if the *Red Herring* finds us first?" asked Oliver.

"There's only one cannon left, mate." The Captain sighed. "We'll just have to hope the sea dogs don't catch up to us."

"I saw a tall iceberg off the starboard side," said Oliver. "I'll go up it and keep watch if you'd like."

"That would be a real help, mate," said the Captain. "I'll have one of the crew row you over in the skiff." He pulled out his small spyglass and a whistle.

"You'd better take these with you. If I hear the whistle, I'll know something's wrong."

"I hope I won't need to blow it!" said Oliver.

Chapter Seven
A Bird's-Eye View

Oliver knew the iceberg would be steep and slippery, so he took along several tacks and some rope to help him climb it. He also packed a small chunk of cheese.

When the slope got too steep for him to keep his footing, he pushed the first tack into the ice. Once it was steady, he pulled himself up onto it and did the same thing over and over again. Huffing and puffing every step of the way, he finally reached a little ledge in the ice. There he stopped for a rest and a tasty bite of cheese.

Oliver gazed out over the sea. He was already higher than the ship's tallest mast. He stared at the top of the iceberg. Still a long way to go. Had he brought enough tacks?

"Wait a minute," he said to himself. "If I lasso that icy spike up there near the top, I could just pull myself up!"

Carefully, he looped the rope and swung it around with all his might. He tossed it toward the icy spike above.

"Got it!" he squeaked. Then he pulled the rope tight and worked his way up. Once he reached the icy spike, he easily climbed the rest of the way.

"What a view!" he exclaimed. "No mist today. I can see for miles!"

He turned his head, looking for any sign of a ship on the sparkling blue waters.

"Too many icebergs," he said to himself. "A ship might be hiding behind any one of them." He sat down. "Oh well, if a ship is moving, it could come out from behind the ice at any minute. I'll just have to keep on looking." He lifted the spyglass to his eye and scanned the horizon.

Suddenly he squeaked, "There's something brown over there in the snow! Is it a ship?" He studied it a minute, "Rocks! Land! . . . The Great Southern Continent! It's here!" he shouted. "We've found it!" At least something good would come out of this voyage.

He was thinking about another bite of cheese when he heard a sound that froze his blood.

"Caw, caw."

It was Barnacle, the sea dogs' parrot! And he was flying this way!

Oliver groaned. "If he sees the *Seven Seas* down there, we'll be in big trouble!"

"Caw, caw, caw."

"What to do?" said Oliver. "Charles would know." He plopped down onto his sack.

"YEEEOWWCH!" he yelled. "I forgot about those tacks!"

"Caw, caw."

"Oh no! Barnacle must have heard me!" whispered Oliver. "He's circling down this way!"

The lasso! He coiled it up and tied the end to a tack that he had stomped into the ice.

Then he swung the loop around, faster and faster.

"Caw, caw, caw!" Barnacle swooped down, his claws outstretched, ready to snatch up the mouse.

Oliver threw the lasso up so hard that he slipped on the ice and fell, sliding down the iceberg's steep slope. But still he held the rope tight. Suddenly he was yanked back up. Barnacle's feet were caught in the ropes. The parrot squawked angrily and tried to fly away.

"Gotcha!" yelled Oliver triumphantly.

The rope went tight. Barnacle squawked and pulled at the rope again and again.

"Sorry, parrot," called Oliver. "You're at the end of your rope!" He glanced at the tack. "I hope—"

Just then the tack popped free of the ice.

"Uh-oh!" Now he was dangling from the rope as the parrot struggled to fly higher and higher into the sky. Oliver held on with all his might.

Barnacle tried to peck at the rope on his feet, but he couldn't get it loose. Then he went into a dive. He was heading right for the top of an iceberg!

"YIKES!" Oliver scrambled up the rope as fast as he could.

Barnacle swooped down like a bomber and pulled up at the last minute. *WHOOOSH!* Oliver just cleared the ice.

He made himself keep inching up the rope. The parrot got set for another dive. But Oliver was so close it didn't matter.

Barnacle kicked at the approaching mouse. Oliver just kept on coming. Suddenly Oliver clutched the bird's feet and wrapped them in two more loops of rope. Barnacle tried to peck at him. Oliver tossed a loop toward the parrot's beak. Missed. He tried again. The rope caught around the bird's lower beak. Oliver pulled back and held it tight. The bird's struggles only made the rope settle deep into his mouth, like a horse's bit.

"Yah!" yelled Oliver. "Now I've really gotcha!" He climbed onto the parrot's back, holding onto the ropes as if they were a horse's reins. Then he pulled up the rest of the rope, coiling it around his arm.

"Have you ever heard of cowboys, Barnacle?" asked Oliver.

"Gwawk!" squawked the angry parrot.

"Well, you've got one riding on you now!" Oliver said. "And just in case you give me any trouble, I've even got myself a spur!" He poked the tack through the back of his shoe.

"Now giddyup, Barney!"

"GWAWK!"

"We're going to look for a couple of ships!"

Oliver pulled back on the parrot's reins.

"Up, Barney!" he called.

"Gwawk!"

"The higher we go, the more we can see," said Oliver. "Too bad I don't have that spyglass with me anymore."

Barnacle circled higher and higher. Oliver could see for miles all around. Off to his left was the coast of the Southern Continent.

Almost directly below, looking like a waterbug on the sea, was the *Seven Seas*. Captain Tabby surely didn't realize how close they were to land.

"Barnacle, I want you to fly me over to the *Red Herring*," said Oliver calmly.

"Caw!"

"And you had better stay high and be quiet," warned Oliver. "In fact, just to make sure . . ." He undid his belt and looped it around Barnacle's beak. "There!"

"Mmmmfff! Mmmmff!" Barnacle shook his head and flew in a dizzying circle.

"If you try any tricks," Oliver said, "you'll be scolded sharply." He tapped the parrot's side with his spur.

The reluctant parrot submitted at last
and turned east. Oliver urged him higher, just
to be sure. After a few minutes' flight, a
tiny-looking ship appeared on the other side of
an iceberg.

"Aha!" Oliver exclaimed. "The *Red
Herring*!" He checked its position carefully.
Actually it wasn't that far from the *Seven Seas*.

The sea dogs would surely have spotted the crippled ship, if it weren't for several icebergs in between. Oliver yanked the reins. "North, Barney! We've got one more ship to find."

"Mmmmfff!" said the parrot. But he obeyed, turning back out toward the open sea.

Chapter Eight
Old Friends

Soon they were approaching the two giant icebergs with the narrow passageway between. Oliver told Barnacle to fly lower.

"Quite a snowball fight we had there," he said. "Maybe I should go down and thank those penguins." They flew closer, and he cheered out loud. "The *Nine Lives*!"

"Mmmff!"

"Don't worry, Barney," said Oliver. "Take us down, and I'll put in a good word for you—even though you didn't mean to help."

Barnacle circled down toward the ship and the group of penguins that had gathered near the shore. In the midst of the curious birds, Oliver thought he could see two cats.

"Take us down there!" said Oliver.

He had Barnacle circle once above the cats before coming in for a landing.

"Admiral, Mr. Calico, it's me!" he squeaked as loudly as he could.

Admiral Winchester jerked around, then looked up at him.

"Oliver!" he exclaimed.

"And Barnacle!" added Mr. Calico, in amazement.

The penguins stared up at Oliver and started asking questions.

"Oliver? Barnacle?"

"What's a barnacle bird?"

"How do you spell that?"

The parrot glided to a landing in front of the two cats. Oliver jumped off and saluted. "At your service, Admiral!" Mr. Calico hurried to secure the parrot.

"Well, Oliver," said the Admiral, "Charles told us you were here, but—"

"Charles?" interrupted Oliver.

"Oliver!" His squeaky voice came from the crowd of penguins.

Now it was Oliver's turn to stare.

Charles scampered over and gave him a hug. "I know what you must have thought, Oliver, but I'm fine!"

"But what—? How could—" Oliver stammered.

"You sound like our penguin friends," chuckled Charles. "One question at a time, please."

"You're alive!" said Oliver.

"Yes," said Charles. "That whale didn't eat me or even drown me. Though I don't think he cared much for me by the time we parted ways."

"What happened?"

"After I fell into the water, I landed on a whale's back. Next thing I knew, I got sucked into the big fellow's blowhole. I was stuck!" said Charles. "After that he must have spouted me out. When I came to my senses, I found myself here! Our good friends, the penguins, have taken excellent care of me."

"It's good to see you alive, friend!" Oliver shook Charles's paw and hugged him again. Then he looked at the cats standing beside them. "Oh yes—Admiral—the *Seven Seas* needs your help," he said.

"Charles told us about the sea dogs' ship," Admiral Winchester said. "I'm sure that the *Seven Seas* and the *Nine Lives* will be up to their challenge."

"I'm afraid it won't be that easy," said Oliver. "The *Seven Seas* is barely staying afloat! The whales hit it."

"Oh, dear!" gasped the Admiral. "Can you lead us to them?"

"Yes," said Oliver. "And thanks to my feathered friend, I know where the *Red Herring* is too. It's at a safe distance for now."

"Mmmmmff!" squawked the parrot.

"He doesn't seem too happy about helping, does he?" said Mr. Calico.

The Admiral chuckled. "Nevertheless, with a few more favors like this, he'll be all parrot and no pirate. Ha, ha!"

The penguins looked puzzled. Everyone else smiled politely.

The Admiral walked over and undid the belt on the parrot's beak. "Listen, Mr. Barnacle, I've got a treasure chest full of dried fruits, Brazil nuts, and roasted sesame seeds. I was planning it as a gift to the Queen. But it's all yours if we can count on your help. I doubt if the pirates treat you so well."

The parrot cocked his head. "Caww?" Oliver thought he looked interested.

Admiral Winchester untied the rope from Barnacle's feet. Oliver watched carefully, but the bird didn't fly away.

"Perhaps we can set a trap for those sea dogs," said the Admiral.

"Another ambush?" asked Perry the penguin.

"A bush?"

"What kind of bush?" asked one of the penguins.

"Yes!" said Charles. "That sounds great! If we can find a good place—an ambush!"

"How about the big ice cave in the rocks?" asked Perry.

"An ice cave?" Oliver smiled.

"Rocks?" The Admiral smiled. "You mean—"

"Oh, yes, Admiral," said Oliver. "I forgot to tell you, I've seen the Great Continent!"

"The Great Continent," repeated the Admiral slowly.

"Continent?" asked a penguin.

"What's a continent?"

"How do you spell it?"

Oliver winked at Charles. "Don't worry, I won't even try it. But can you show us where this cave is, Perry?"

"Certainly," Perry said. "That is, if you'll take us with you to help."

"Oh, yes!" cheered the penguins.

"Sounds like an excellent idea," said the Admiral. "But first we must rescue the crew of the *Seven Seas*! Back to the ship, Mr. Calico!"

"Aye, aye, sir!" answered the first mate.

The two cats, the two mice, and about three dozen penguins boarded the *Nine Lives* and prepared to set sail again. The crew was surprised to see all the volunteers, especially one very familiar-looking parrot.

Oliver studied the map with the Admiral.

"Here's where we need to go," said Oliver. He pointed to a spot on the map. "But it sure was a lot easier to fly over all those icebergs."

"Take up anchor, Mr. Calico. We'll bear left at the passage ahead," called the Admiral. "And do keep an eye on that parrot in my cabin."

"Aye, aye, sir," said the first mate.

The *Nine Lives* sailed through the fields of ice for nearly an hour. Then, as the great ship slid around an iceberg, Oliver cried out, "There it is! The *Seven Seas!*"

"And still afloat," added Admiral Winchester happily.

Mr. Calico steered the *Nine Lives* over toward the crippled ship. Soon the two ships floated side by side. The happy crew of the *Seven Seas* eagerly boarded the Admiral's ship.

They all shook each other's paws and laughed with joy at their rescue. Captain Tabby seemed the happiest of all, especially when he greeted Charles. The penguins got so excited that they did a waddling sort of jig on the deck. Once the celebration had died down, the Admiral told Captain Tabby about their plan.

"Sounds excellent!" exclaimed the Captain. "It would be nice to turn the tables on those sea dogs again."

"I thought you might like it," said the Admiral. "Maybe we can teach those old sea dogs some new tricks. Ha, ha."

Captain Tabby smiled. "I'll be glad to contribute some equipment from the *Seven Seas* to help in the ambush. I'm afraid she won't be sailing any longer herself." He looked sadly at his patched-up ship.

Admiral Winchester patted his friend on the back. "Thank you, Tabby."

The crew cut down sails and rigging from the *Seven Seas*. They carried off pulleys, barrels, and coils of rope from the damaged ship. The last thing they brought was the ship's tattered flag.

"What are you going to do with all that stuff?" asked Perry.

"You'll see, once the fun starts," said Oliver with a smile.

"You just take us to the cave," said Charles.

Chapter Nine
Setting the Trap

As soon as the *Nine Lives* was loaded, they set sail toward the Great Ice Cave. As Oliver helped direct Mr. Calico through the icebergs, Charles and the Admiral stood nearby, peering around each iceberg they passed. They were hoping for their first glance of the legendary Great Southern Continent.

"I'm glad you two good mice decided to come after all," said Admiral Winchester. "Just think what you would have missed."

Charles looked at Oliver. Oliver looked back at him. "I'm thinking," Oliver said quietly.

"Land ho!" came a sailor's call from the mast. And suddenly the rocky, icy shore came into sight.

"The Great Southern Continent!" exclaimed Admiral Winchester. "We shall not disappoint the Queen after all."

"Let's hope we can still disappoint the sea dogs," said Charles.

When the *Nine Lives* had dropped anchor, the ship's officers and the two mice rowed to shore. Then the Admiral gave a speech. Captain Tabby planted the Queen's flag in the ice. As soon as the ceremony ended, they started work on setting up the ambush.

"Come now, mates," called Mr. Calico. "On to the cave! And bring along the leftover equipment from the *Seven Seas*."

The crew carried ropes, pulleys, and sails on shore. Near the end of the line came Barnacle the parrot. The penguins led them through the snow to the Great Ice Cave.

When they arrived, Admiral Winchester lit his lantern and stepped inside the narrow opening to the cave. "This is a perfect place for an ambush," he said.

"Once we seal off the entrance, there will be no escape!" Captain Tabby said with a smile.

"Let's start setting up our traps!" said Charles and Oliver together.

"There's lots of iceballs in the back of the cave," said Perry with a twinkle in his eye. "Let's go get them!"

The other penguins clucked with excitement. "Oh yes, iceballs!"

"We love throwing iceballs!"

"I can spell that. I-c-e-b-a-l-l-s."

Charles and Oliver laughed as the penguins waddled to the back of the dimly lit cave. Meanwhile, the sailors had started stringing up pulleys and rigging along the icy walls.

"Oliver," said Admiral Winchester. "Are you ready for another ride on Barnacle's back?"

"Sure," said Oliver.

"Fly over to the *Red Herring*, and when you get above them, have the parrot squawk to get their attention," said the Admiral. "Then fly back this way. They'll follow you right into our trap."

"And they won't suspect a thing as long as you stay out of sight," said Charles.

"Right," said the Admiral. "Just keep that parrot high enough, and they'll never see you."

"Where is Barney anyway?" asked Oliver.

"I've been keeping an eye on him," called Mr. Calico. "He's over here."

"Be careful," said Charles. "I still don't trust that bird."

"Oh, I certainly will," said Oliver. "For Barney's encouragement, I brought a little dried fruit in my pocket. Besides, I've still got my 'cowboy spur.' " He smiled and stuck the tack through the back of his shoe again.

"Now I'm all set," he said. He got his rope, hopped onto Barnacle's back, and looped the rope into the parrot's beak. "Well, Barney, let's head for the *Red Herring*," he said. "It's time to round up some sea dogs!"

The parrot took off and climbed high into the clear sky. Oliver glanced back at the *Nine Lives*, anchored near the ice cave. "It's a great trap," said Oliver. "Now it's all up to us, Barn—"

"Caw!" the parrot squawked angrily. He flipped upsidedown. The rope fell out of his beak and Oliver lost his grip. Before he knew what was happening, Oliver was falling head over heels toward the icy sea below.

He felt himself snatched out of midair. The parrot's sharp claws were digging into his fur. He squirmed back and forth, but it was no use. He was Barnacle's prisoner now.

"Caw! Caw! Caw!" Was that parrot laughing?

"I thought you were trying to drown me!" yelled Oliver.

"Caw!" The parrot shook his head.

"Of course not," said Oliver. "You're taking me back to Crag, aren't you?"

"Caw! Caw!"

"Well, he's not going to get anything out of me!" said Oliver defiantly. "And you can't talk!"

"Caw!"

"You might as well drop me into the sea!"

To himself, Oliver muttered, "I'd stand a better chance in the water!"

But Barnacle was circling down toward the *Red Herring*. "Well lookey-ear, mates!" yelled Captain Crag. "Barney's back—an' 'es brought us a prize! It's a fine, fat mouse."

Oliver tried to keep from trembling as Barnacle dropped him into the pirate captain's paw.

"Why I believes we've met before, 'ave we?" growled Crag with a wicked smile on his face.

Suddenly Oliver heard a *rat-tat-tatting* on the deck. O'Grady's wooden leg was tapping with excitement. "It's that fat rat, ain't it Cap'n," said the grizzled sea dog. "The one what bit me toe back on the *Herring Bone!*"

"An' 'elped them cats o' the *Nine Lives* ta get away from us back at San Fiero," added Big Tom.

"Aye, mates," growled the Captain. " 'Es the one all right! An' I reckon it means that the *Nine Lives* can't be far away!"

"Caw! Caw!"

"Now, mousie," Captain Crag continued, "maybe you'd be so kind as ta tell us whar tha *Nine Lives* be?"

"Caw!" Barnacle flapped his wings.

"What's yer problem, Barney?" growled Big Tom. "Ye ain't afraid of them cats, are ya? Maybe yer half-chicken!" All the sea dogs laughed, except for O'Grady.

"Barney ain't afraid of nothin'," said O'Grady, scowling.

Barnacle puffed out his chest feathers and flew to O'Grady's shoulder.

Oliver squeaked, "He looked mighty afraid to me when Admiral Win—Oh!" He clapped his paw over his mouth.

Crag narrowed his eyes and pulled Oliver to within an inch of his nose. "So ye been with the good Adm'ral, eh?"

"Did I say that?" asked Oliver.

Crag squeezed Oliver until he gasped for air. "Don't play games with me, mousie. Yer gonna lead us ta the *Nine Lives*, an' yer gonna do it now, see?" Crag breathed his smelly hot breath into Oliver's face.

Oliver coughed. "Aye, aye, Cap'n."

But Barnacle flapped his wings again and shook his head. "Caw! Caw! Caw!"

"Shut yer beak, ya half-chicken excuse fer a parrot!" growled Big Tom.

Barnacle flew at Tom's face, flapping his wings and squawking wildly. All the sea dogs laughed. Finally the big dog managed to catch the parrot by the neck.

"*Squawk!*"

Tom grabbed the bandana off O'Grady's head. He wrapped Barnacle up in it, tied it together with six different sailor's knots, and handed it back to the peg-legged pirate. "Maybe ya can manage yer bird better now, O'Grady," he growled.

"Mmmfff! mmmmfff!" Barnacle squawked from inside the bandana. But the knots were so tight, O'Grady couldn't get them loose. Soon the whole ship of sea dogs was barking with laughter.

"Now, mousie," said Crag, "lead us to whar the *Nine Lives* might be."

Oliver nodded, trying not to show his relief. The trap was set. Barnacle couldn't give anything away. It was almost too easy.

Chapter Ten
To the Cave

Before long, with Oliver's help, Crag spotted the *Nine Lives* at anchor.

A sea dog with a telescope called down from the crow's-nest. "She looks ta be deserted, Cap'n."

"Pull in close, an' we'll take us a look," said Crag. When they got closer, he pointed to the flag on shore. "Ain't that precious, mates," he sneered. "They claimed the Continent fer thar dear Queenie."

"Maybe they's lookin' fer treasure, Cap'n," said one sea dog.

"Har, har, wouldn't that be good timin', eh, mates?" said Crag. "Let's get ashore. Maybe we ken give them cats a little surprise."

"Mmmmff! mmmmmfff!"

Oliver looked at the squirming bandana and thought about the ambush. He almost smiled.

Just then Crag barked out an order. "Big Tom, get yerself another bandana an' stuff this mouse in it. I'm keepin' 'im in me pocket, an' I won't 'ave no squeakin' ta spoil ar surprise."

The next thing he knew, Oliver was inside a dark bandana folded over four times and tied in more knots than he could count. "Guess I'd better start chewing," he said to himself. He could hear the splashing of oars in water. They must be rowing to shore.

Soon he was bouncing around in Crag's pocket again. Snow crunched beneath the bulldog's feet.

"Now ain't this easy, mates," said Crag. "Footprints in the snow."

"Even a bird-brain like O'Grady could find them cats this a way," said Big Tom.

O'Grady snarled.

"Mmmfff!" squawked Barnacle.

"Come on, mates," growled Crag. "An' keep it quiet now."

By now, Oliver had nibbled a hole in the bandana. It was just big enough for him to squeeze his head through. Crag stopped. "A cave," the Captain whispered. "C'mon, mates, follow me."

Still wrapped in the bandana, Oliver poked his head out of Crag's pocket. It was dark. They must be inside the cave.

THWAP! Whizzzzz! THWAP! THWAP!

From all sides, iceballs pelted down upon them. The penguins had attacked.

Oliver ducked down deep into the pocket.

"It's an ambush," yelled Crag. "Get out!"

Some of the sea dogs turned and headed back toward the entrance. Oliver peeked out again.

Thwop! A net made of rope rigging fell over the pirates, blocking the way out. Then a sloshing sound filled the cave as barrels of icy water were spilled onto the cave's floor. Almost instantly, the water froze into a thin layer of ice.

Sea dogs slipped and slid into each other.

"Ooooof!"

"Aaaargh!"

"Mmmmff!"

Oliver rocked back and forth in Crag's pocket. He clung to the bandana and waited.

The rusty pulleys squeaked and cranked overhead. A wave of sharp icicles showered down from a sail near the ceiling.

"Yeeowch!"

"Eeeyikes!"

"Mmmmff! mmmmff!"

Thump! Crag must have fallen down too.

Oliver used his teeth to pull himself out of Crag's pocket.

"I'm on the wrong side of this ambush!" he muttered. "I'm getting out of here!" Still knotted into the bandana, he bumped and wiggled away from the pile of snarling sea dogs.

Swiiishhh! Swiiiiishh!

"What next?" Oliver wondered. His eyes were used to the dim light, now, and he looked all around.

SWOOOSH! A cat-sailor on skis passed right over him, one leg on each side. The skiing sailor and his mate skied right toward the biggest pile of sea dogs, each cat holding the end of a rope.

They circled around the pirates once, twice, three times, wrapping them up tightly with the rope. Then the snow spray from their skis swished over Oliver, and he could see no more.

"Lights, please," said Admiral Winchester.

The lanterns glowed. Along the cave walls stood cat-sailors with their swords drawn. Between them stood penguins with their iceballs in hand.

"Well, Crag," asked the Admiral. "Will you surrender? We have you surrounded, and most of your crew is already tied up!"

Crag stood up slowly. He patted his pocket, then he looked down by his feet and snatched up a knotted bandana that was nearly covered with snow. The old pirate captain smiled his most wicked smile.

"Thar is another matter ta consider," he growled. "And that's the contents of this 'ere bandana." He dangled the bandana around for all to see.

"What are you talking about, Crag?"

"Why it's yer little mousie friend it is," snarled the bulldog. "An' if ye don't warnt ta see me squeeze the life outa him, now, maybe ye might warnta let us sea dogs go free, see?"

"Oliver?" gasped Charles.

Admiral Winchester paused.

"Har, har, har," laughed Crag. Then he gave the bandana a little squeeze so all could hear the mouse squeak.

"Mmmmff!"

Crag looked puzzled.

"That doesn't sound like Oliver," said Charles slowly.

Crag ripped open the bandana.

"SQUAWK!"

"Barnacle?" gasped Crag.

Then from a snowy pile several feet away came a faint voice. "Admiral—it's me, Oliver! I'm fine! Just get me out of this bandana!"

Immediately the cats closed in and tied up Crag and the rest of the sea dogs. Charles ran over to Oliver and helped get him out of the cloth. Then they hugged and congratulated each other.

"Great ambush," said Oliver. "Wish I'd been on the other side of it." He rubbed a bruise on his head.

"It wouldn't have been much of an ambush if you hadn't invited our guests of honor," Charles said, looking over at the pile of grumbling sea dogs. "I'm sorry about your head, though."

"Those iceballs are awfully hard," said Oliver. He reached down and picked up one. "Look at this, Charles. It almost looks like some kind of colored rock."

Charles took the iceball from Oliver. He scratched at its frosty surface. Then he scurried over to a nearby lantern.

"What is it, Charles?" squeaked Oliver. He hurried after his friend.

"Perry!" called Charles to the penguin. "Where did you get these iceballs?"

Perry waddled over. "In the back of the cave—there are boxes full of them!"

"These aren't iceballs, Perry," said Charles. "They're jewels!"

"Jewels?" asked Perry

"Jewels!" said Oliver.

"How do you spell that?" asked another penguin.

The news spread quickly. The Admiral's crew hauled six treasure chests from the back of the cave. Charles and Oliver scrambled up the side of one chest and jumped inside. They were swimming in rubies and diamonds, emeralds and sapphires. The jewels sparkled in the flickering lantern light.

"Some kind of iceballs, eh Oliver," said Charles with a laugh.

"The legendary treasures of the ice!" exclaimed Admiral Winchester.

"Unbelievable!" said Captain Tabby.

"You can have them if you like," said Perry.

The cats gasped.

"Do you know how much this is worth?" asked Charles.

"I hope it's enough to buy you a new ship once you get back home." Perry looked at Captain Tabby.

Captain Tabby laughed. "More than enough, my good friend."

"Would it buy us a trip to England, too?" asked Perry.

"Most certainly!" replied the Admiral. "You are welcome to join us!"

The penguins all cheered and did a waddling jig.

"There is one problem with that idea," said Oliver suddenly.

"What's that?" asked Perry.

"Well," said Oliver, "it does get rather warm up there."

At that the whole crew laughed.

"Oliver," said Charles. "You've been here toooo long! It's time for us to go home."

And so it was. Before the icy mist had settled on the Great Southern Continent even one more time, the *Nine Lives* and the *Red Herring* (under new command) set sail northward. They returned to England with a crew of happy cats, curious penguins, growling pirate-prisoners—and two brave mice with a hundred and one stories to tell.